Edward Lear

More Nonsense

pictures, rhymes, botany, etc.

Edward Lear

More Nonsense
pictures, rhymes, botany, etc.

ISBN/EAN: 9783337262464

Printed in Europe, USA, Canada, Australia, Japan

Cover: Foto ©Andreas Hilbeck / pixelio.de

More available books at **www.hansebooks.com**

MORE NONSENSE PICTURES, RHYMES, BOTANY, &c.

MORE NONSENSE,

PICTURES, RHYMES,

BOTANY, ETC.

BY

EDWARD LEAR.

LONDON:
ROBERT JOHN BUSH, 32, CHARING CROSS, S.W.
1872.

Printed by Watson & Hazell, London and Aylesbury.

INTRODUCTION.

In offering this little Book—the third of its kind—to the Public, I am glad to take the opportunity of recording the pleasure I have received at the appreciation its predecessors have met with, as attested by their wide circulation, and by the universally kind notices of them from the Press. To have been the means of administering innocent mirth to thousands, may surely be a just motive for satisfaction, and an excuse for grateful expression.

At the same time, I am desirous of adding a few words as to the history of the two previously published volumes, and more particularly of the first or original " Book of Nonsense," relating to which many absurd reports have crept into circulation, such as that it was the composition of the late Lord Brougham, the late Earl of Derby, &c.; that the rhymes and pictures are by different persons; or that the whole have a symbolical meaning, &c., &c.; whereas, every one of the Rhymes was composed by myself, and every one of the Illustrations drawn by my own hand at the time the verses were made. Moreover, in no portion of these Nonsense drawings have I ever allowed any caricature of private or public persons to appear, and throughout, more care than might be supposed has been given to make the subjects incapable of misinterpretation: "Nonsense," pure and absolute, having been my aim throughout.

As for the persistently absurd report of the late Earl of Derby being the author of the "First Book of Nonsense," I may relate an incident which occurred to me four summers ago, the first that gave me any insight into the origin of the rumour.

I was on my way from London to Guildford, in a railway carriage, containing, besides myself, one passenger, an elderly gentleman:—presently, however, two ladies entered, accompanied by two little boys. These, who had just had a copy of the "Book of Nonsense" given them, were loud in their delight, and by degrees infected the whole party with their mirth

"How grateful," said the old gentleman to the two ladies, "all children and parents too ought to be to the statesman who has given his time to composing that charming book!"

(The ladies looked puzzled, as indeed was I, the Author.)

"Do you not know who is the writer of it?" asked the gentleman.

" The name is ' Edward Lear,' " said one of the ladies.

" Ah!" said the first speaker; "so it is printed, but that is only a whim of the real author, the Earl of Derby. ' Edward' is his christian name, and, as you may see, LEAR is only EARL transposed."

" But," said the lady, doubtingly, "here is a dedication to the great-grand-children, grand-nephews, and grand-nieces of Edward, thirteenth Earl of Derby, by the author, Edward Lear."

" That," replied the other, "is simply a piece of mystification; I am in a position to know that the whole book was composed and illustrated by Lord Derby himself. In fact, there is no such a person at all as Edward Lear."

" Yet," said the other lady, "some friends of mine tell me they know Mr. Lear."

" Quite a mistake! completely a mistake!" said the old gentleman, becoming rather angry at the contradiction, " I am well aware of what I am saying: I can inform you, no such a person as ' Edward Lear' exists!"

Hitherto I had kept silence, but as my hat was, as well as my handkerchief and stick, largely marked inside with my name, and, as I happened to have in my pocket several letters addressed to me, the temptation was too great to resist, so, flashing all these articles at once on my would-be extinguisher's attention, I speedily reduced him to silence.

The second volume of Nonsense, commencing with the verses, " The Owl and the Pussy Cat," was written at different times; and for different sets of children: the whole being collected in the course of last year, were then illustrated, and published in a single volume, by Mr. R. J. Bush, of 32, Charing Cross.

The contents of the third or present volume were made also at different intervals in the last two years.

Long years ago, in days when much of my time was passed in a Country House, where children and mirth abounded, the lines beginning, " There was an old man of Tobago," were suggested to me by a valued friend, as a form of verse lending itself to limitless variety for Rhymes and Pictures ; and thenceforth the greater part of the original drawings and verses for the first " Book of Nonsense" were struck off with a pen, no assistance ever having been given me in any way but that of uproarious delight and welcome at the appearance of every new absurdity.

Most of these Drawings and Rhymes were transferred to lithographic stones in the year 1846, and were then first published by Mr. Thomas McLean, of the Haymarket.   But that edition having been soon exhausted, and the call for the " Book of Nonsense" continuing, I added a considerable number of subjects to those previously published, and having caused the whole to be carefully reproduced in woodcuts, by Messrs. Dalzell, I disposed of the Copyright to Messrs. Routledge and Warne, by whom the volume was published in 1843.

EDWARD LEAR.

VILLA EMILY,
    SAN REMO, AUGUST, 1871.

CONTENTS.

———◆———

NONSENSE BOTANY.

Enkoopia Chickabiddia.

Washtubbia Circularis.

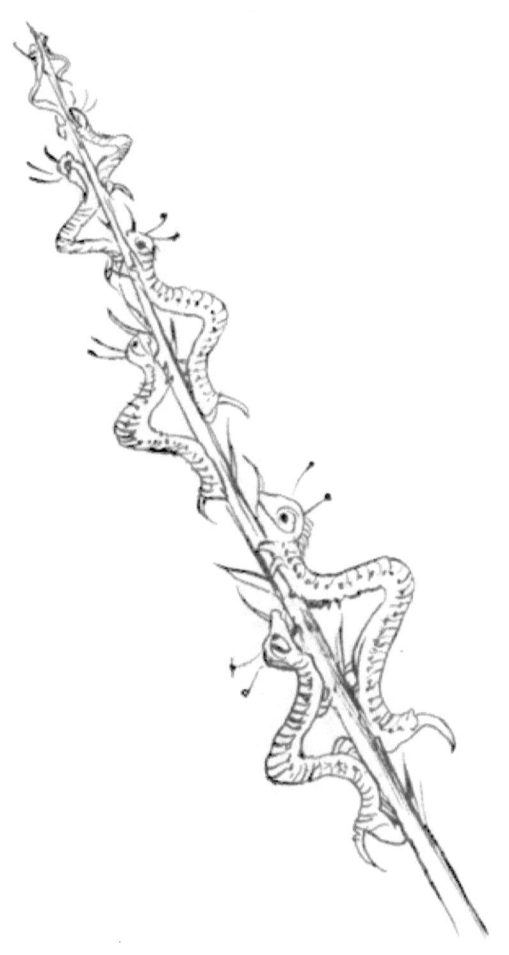

Nasticreechia Krorluppia.

Minspysia Deliciosa.

Barkia Howlaloudia.

Tigerlillia Terribilis.

Tickia Orologica.

Shoebootia Utilis.

The Fizzgiggious Fish,
who always walked about upon Stilts.
because he had no legs.

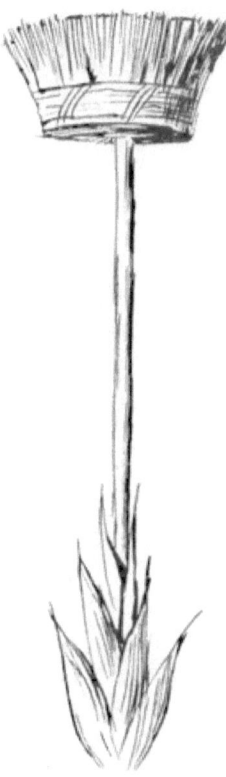

Arthbroomia Rigida.

Jinglia Tinkettlia.

Sophtsluggia Glutinosa.

ONE HUNDRED NONSENSE PICTURES AND RHYMES.

There was an old person of Pisa,
Whose daughters did nothing to please her;
She dressed them in gray, and banged them all day,
Round the walls of the city of Pisa.

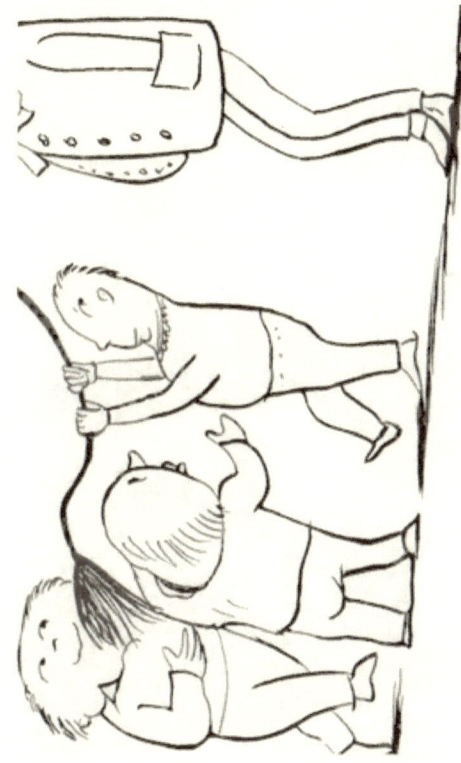

There was an old person of Cassel,
Whose nose finished off in a tassel;
But they call'd out, "Oh well!—don't it look like a bell!"
Which perplexed that old person of Cassel.

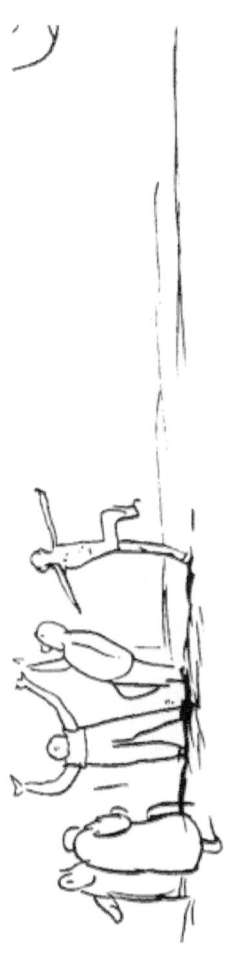

There is a young lady, whose nose,
Continually prospers and grows;
When it grew out of sight, she exclaimed in a fright,
"Oh! Farewell to the end of my nose!"

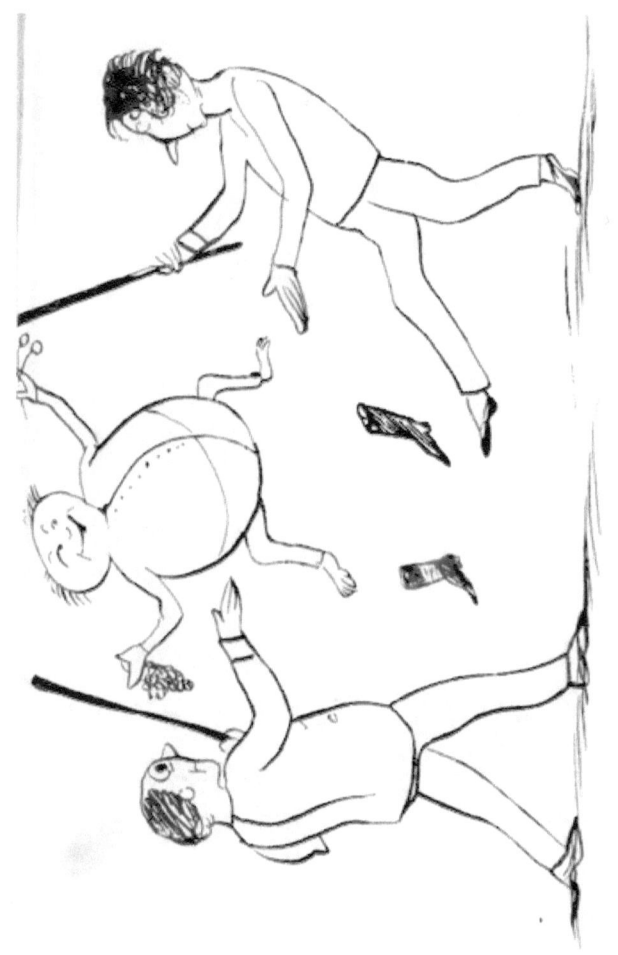

There was an old man who screamed out
Whenever they knocked him about;
So they took off his boots, And fed him with fruits
And continued to knock him about.

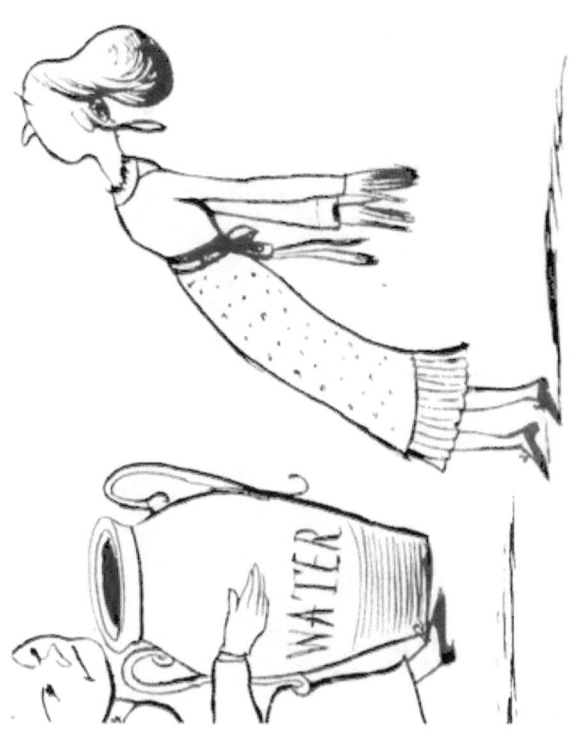

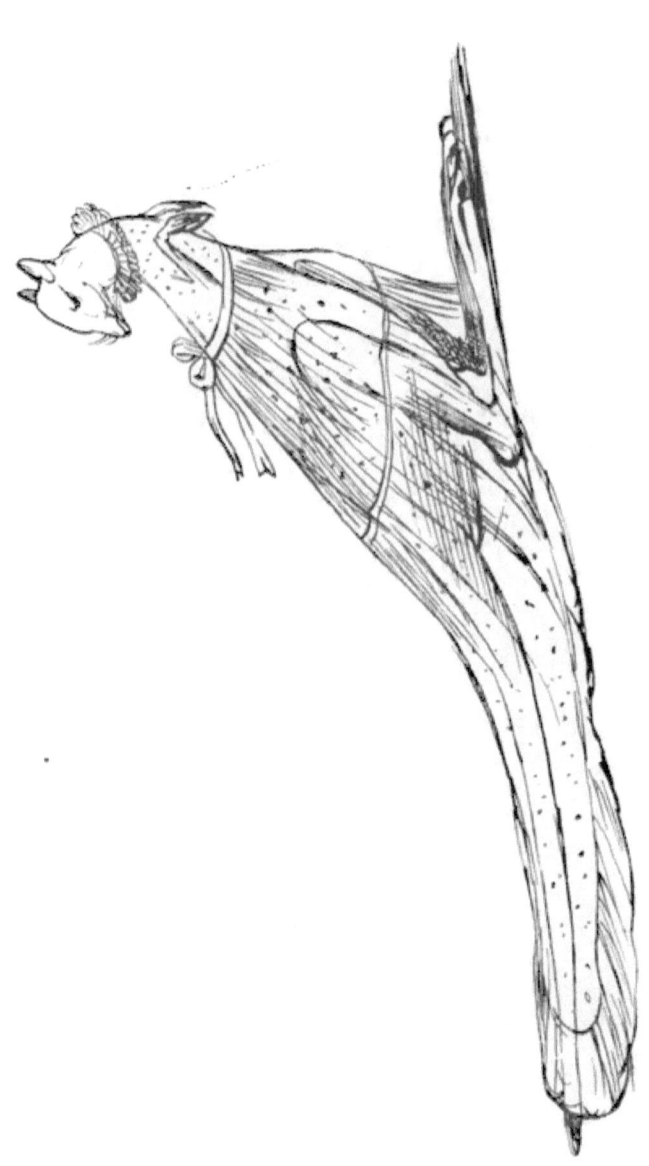

There was an old man of Three Bridges,
Whose mind was distracted by midges,
He sate on a wheel, eating underdone veal,
Which relieved that old man of Three Bridges.

There was an old person of Blythe,
Who cut up his meat with a scythe;
When they said, "Well! I never!" — he cried, "Scythes for ever!"
That lively old person of Blythe.

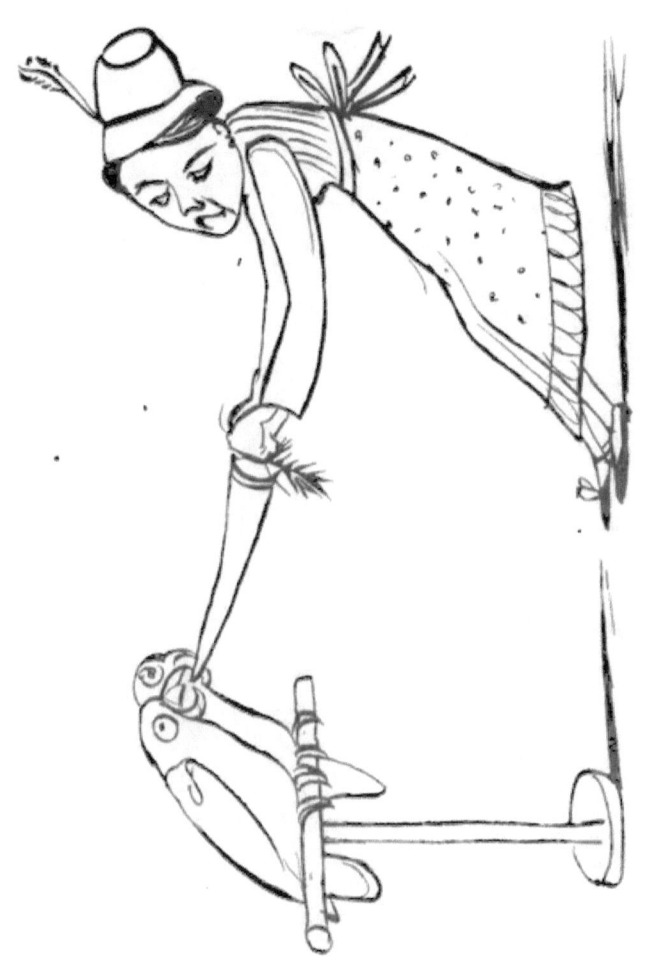

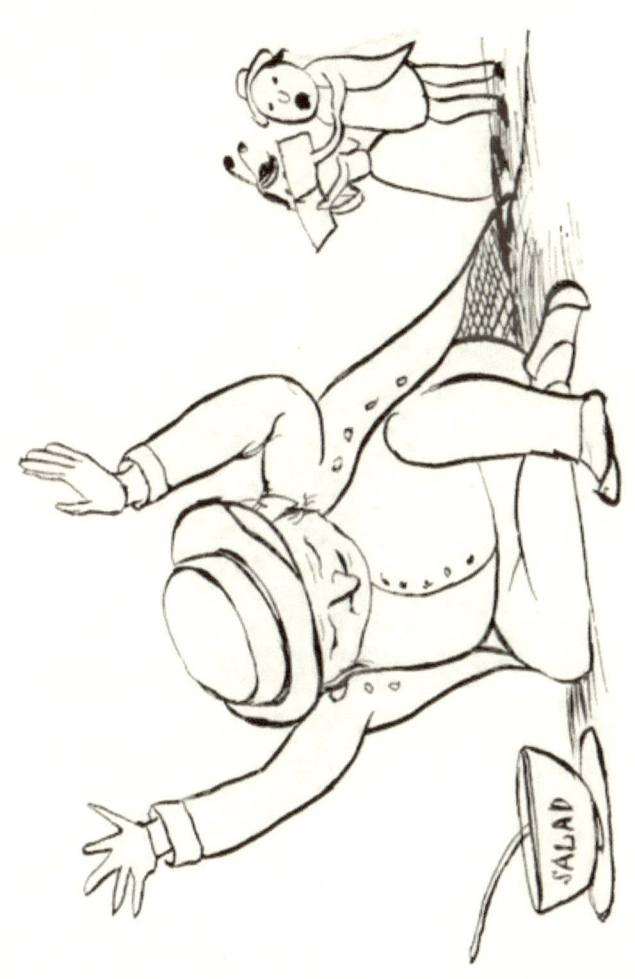

There was an old person of Minety,
Who purchased five hundred and ninety
Large apples and pears, which he threw unawares,
At the heads of the people of Minety.

The Excellent Double-extra XX imbibing King Xerxes, who lived a long while ago.

Stunnia Dinnerbellia.

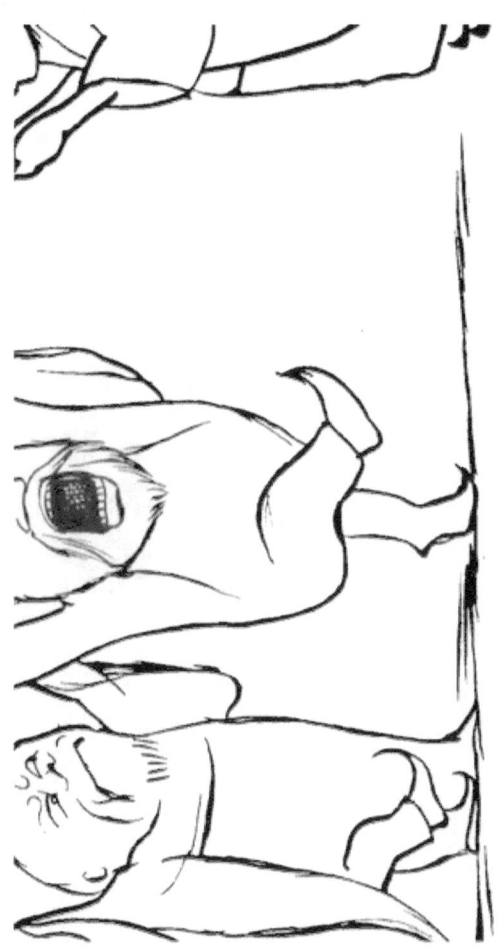

There was an old man of Ibreem,
Who suddenly threaten'd to scream :
But they said, " If you do, we will thump you quite blue,
You disgusting old man of Ibreem!"

There was an old man of Thames Ditton,
Who called out for something to sit on :
But they brought him a hat, and said ——"Sit upon that,
You abruptious old man of Thames Ditton !"

There was an old man in a barge,
Whose nose was exceedingly large;
But in fishing by night, It supported a light,
Which helped that old man in a barge.

There was an old person of Loo,
Who said, " What on earth shall I do?"
When they said, " Go away!"— she continued to stay,
That vexatious old person of Loo.

There was an old man of Thermopylæ,
Who never did anything properly;
But they said, "If you choose, To boil eggs in your shoes,
You shall never remain in Thermopylæ,"

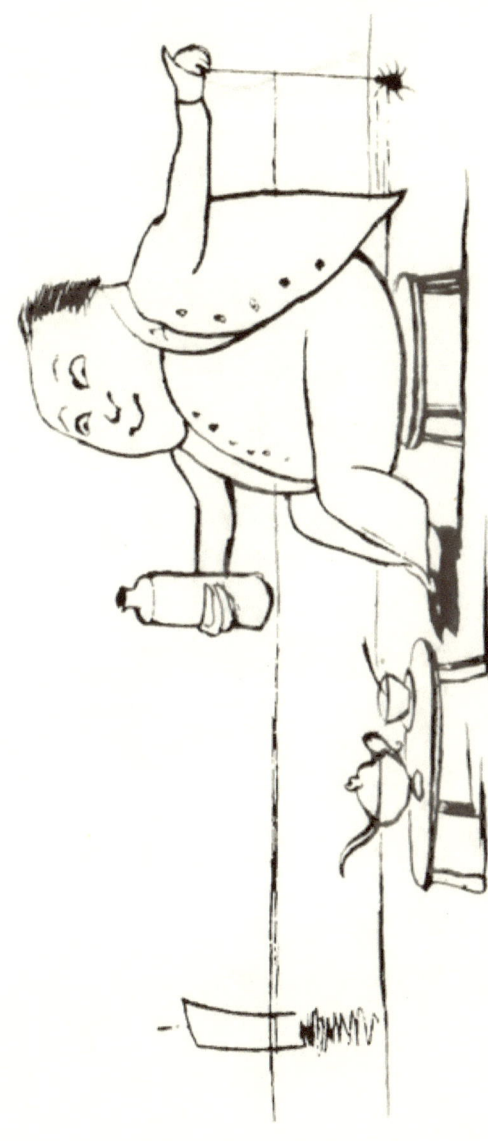

There was an old person of Putney,
Whose food was roast spiders and chutney,
Which he took with his tea, within sight of the sea,
That romantic old person of Putney.

There was an old man whose remorse,
Induced him to drink Caper Sauce;
For they said, "If mixed up, with some cold claret-cup,
It will certainly soothe your remorse!"

There was an old man at a Station,
Who made a promiscuous oration;
But they said, "Take some snuff!—You have talk'd quite enough,
You afflicting old man at a Station!"

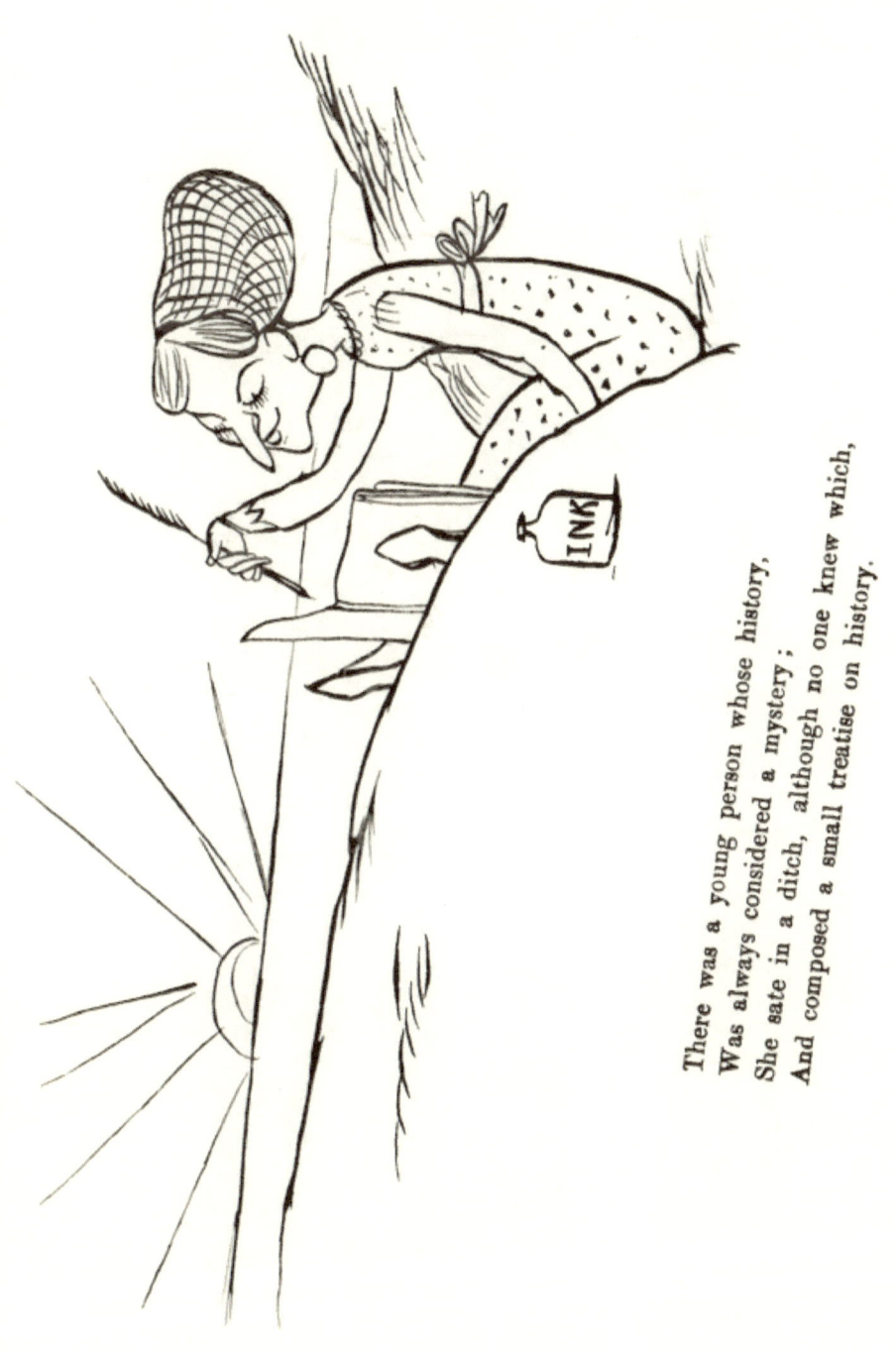

There was a young person whose history,
Was always considered a mystery;
She sate in a ditch, although no one knew which,
And composed a small treatise on history.

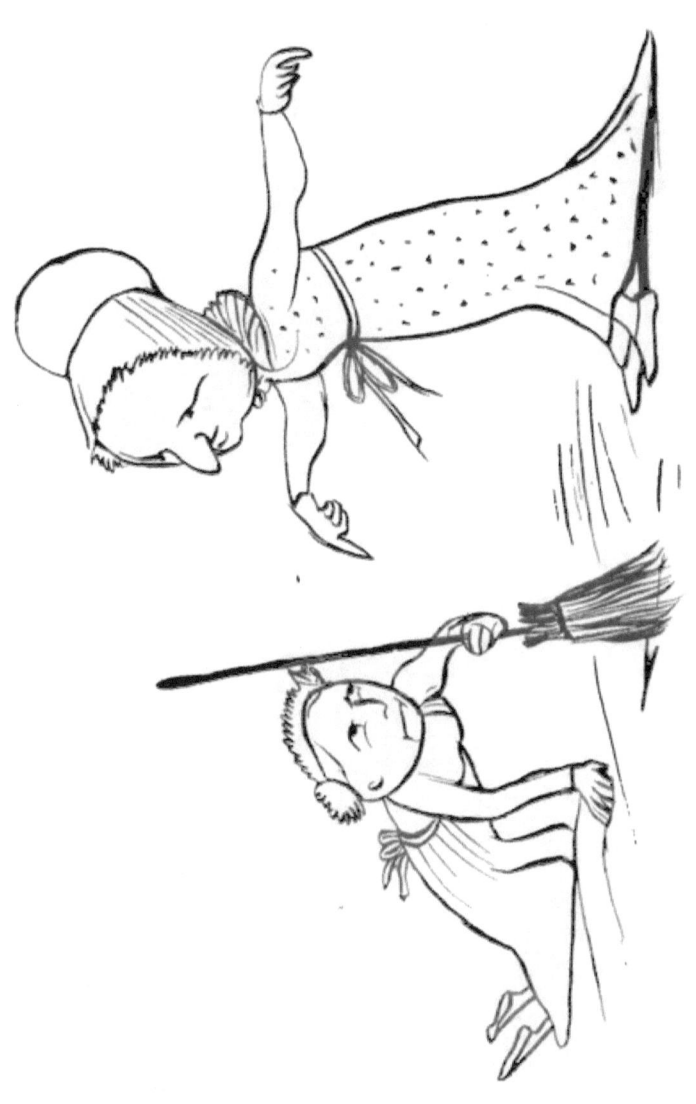

There was an old person of Down,
Whose face was adorned with a frown;
When he opened the door, for one minute or more,
He alarmed all the people of Down.

There was an old person of Bude,
Whose deportment was vicious and crude ;
He wore a large ruff, of pale straw-colored stuff,
Which perplexed all the people of Bude,

There was an old man on the Humber,
Who dined on a cake of Burnt Uumber;
When he said — "It's enough!"—They only said, "Stuff!
You amazing old man on the Humber!"

There was an old man of Dee-side
Whose hat was exceedingly wide,
But he said "Do not fail, If it happen to hail
To come under my hat at Dee-side!"

.

The Absolutely Abstemious Ass,
who resided in a Barrel, and only lived on
Soda Water and Pickled Cucumbers.

There was an old person of Ealing,
Who was wholly devoid of good feeling;
He drove a small gig, with three Owls and a Pig,
Which distressed all the people of Ealing.

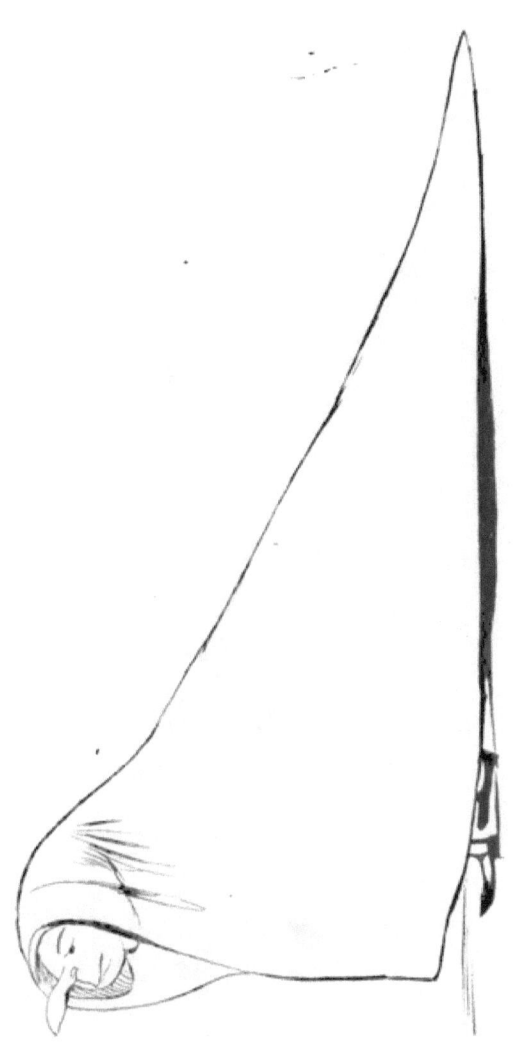

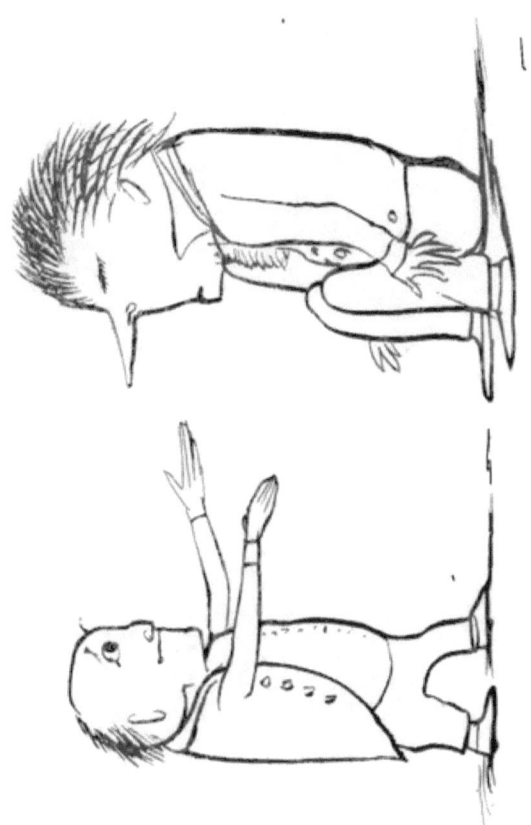

There was an old man of Port Grigor,
Whose actions were noted for vigour;
He stood on his head, till his waistcoat turned red,
That eclectic old man of Port Grigor.

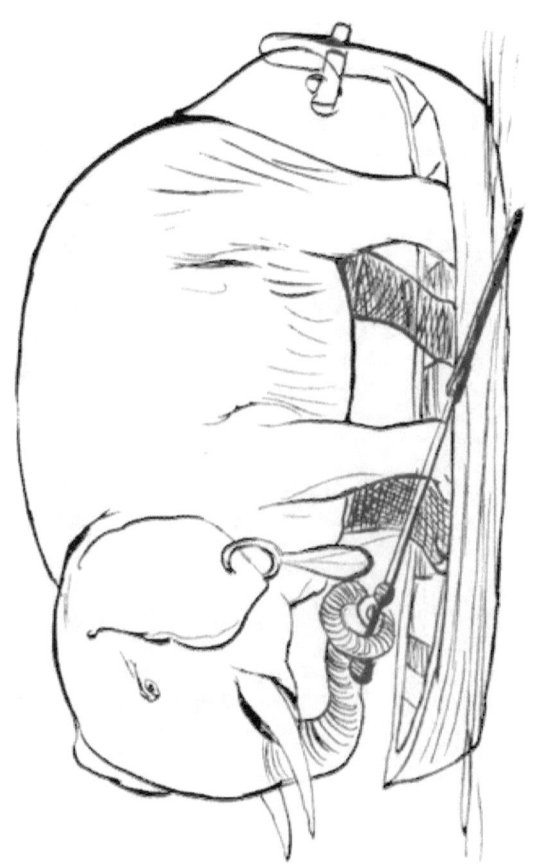

The Enthusiastic Elephant,
who ferried himself across the water with the
Kitchen Poker and a New pair of Ear-rings.

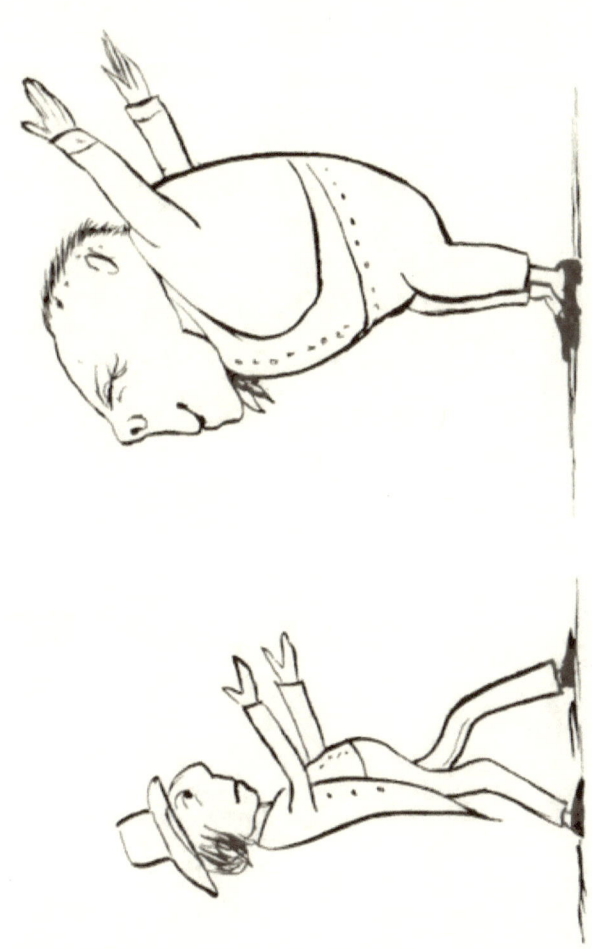
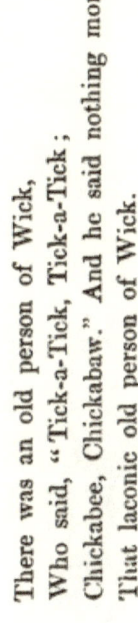

There was an old person of Wick,
Who said, "Tick-a-Tick, Tick-a-Tick;
Chickabee, Chickabaw." And he said nothing more,
That laconic old person of Wick.

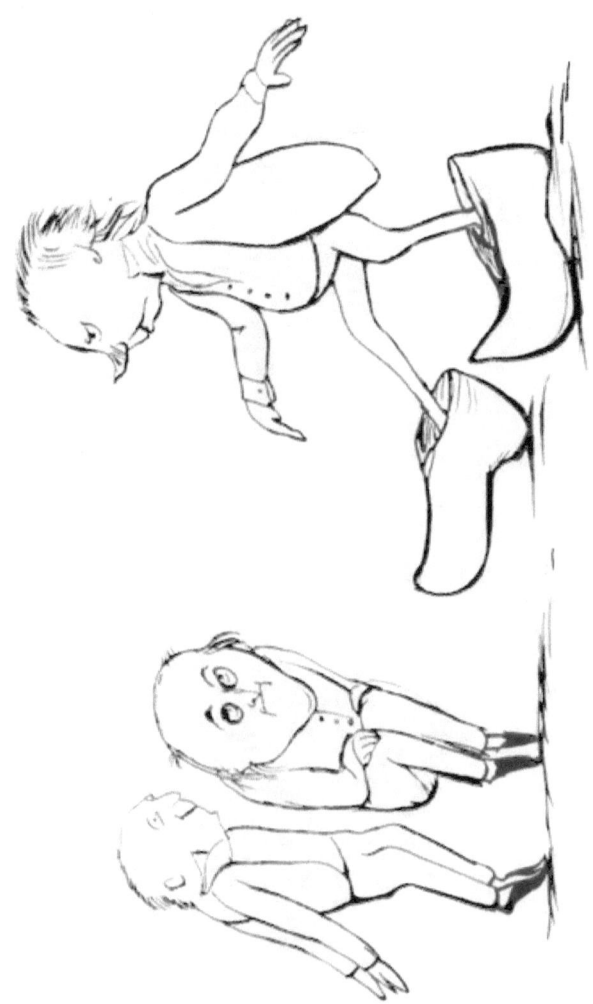

There was an old man of Spithead,
Who opened the window, and said,—
"Fil-jomble, fil-jumble, Fil-rumble-come-tumble!"
That doubtful old man of Spithead.

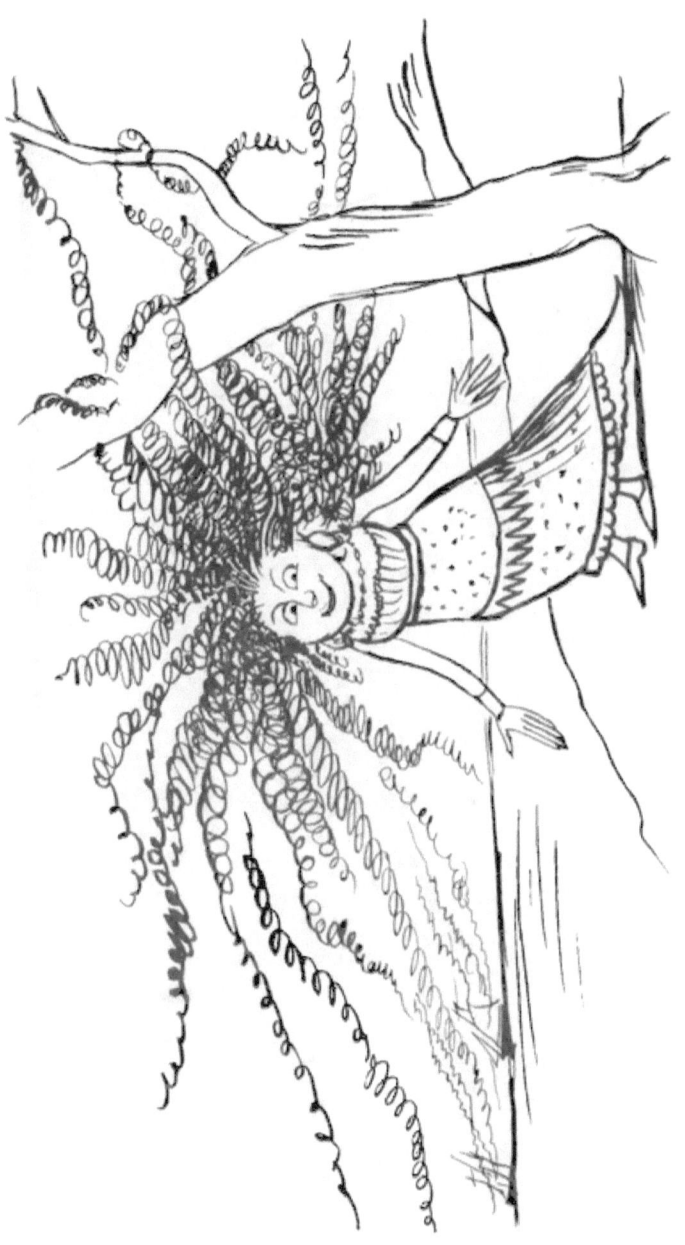

There was a young person of Bantry,
Who frequently slept in the pantry ;
When disturbed by the mice, She appeased them with rice
That judicious young person of Bantry.

There was a young lady of Corsica,
Who purchased a little brown saucy-cur :
Which she fed upon ham, and hot raspberry jam,
That expensive young lady of Corsica.

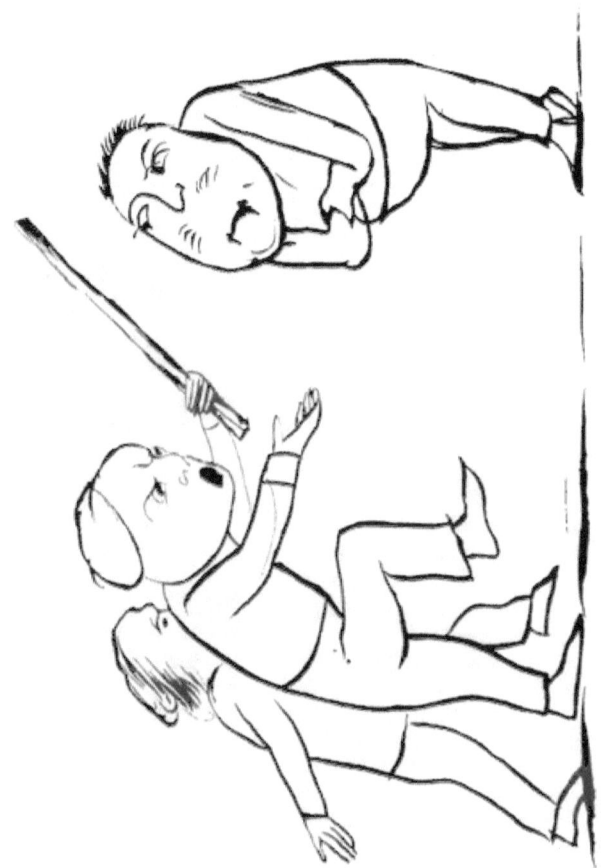

There was an old person of Sark,
Who made an unpleasant remark;
But they said, "Don't you see what a brute you must be!"
You obnoxious old person of Sark.

The Umbrageous Umbrella-maker,
whose Face nobody ever saw, because it was
always covered by his Umbrella.

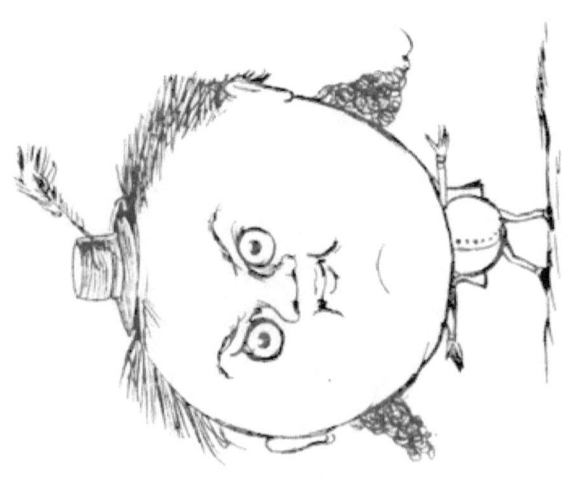

The Yonghy-Bonghy-Bo,
whose Head was ever so much bigger than his
Body, and whose Hat was rather small.

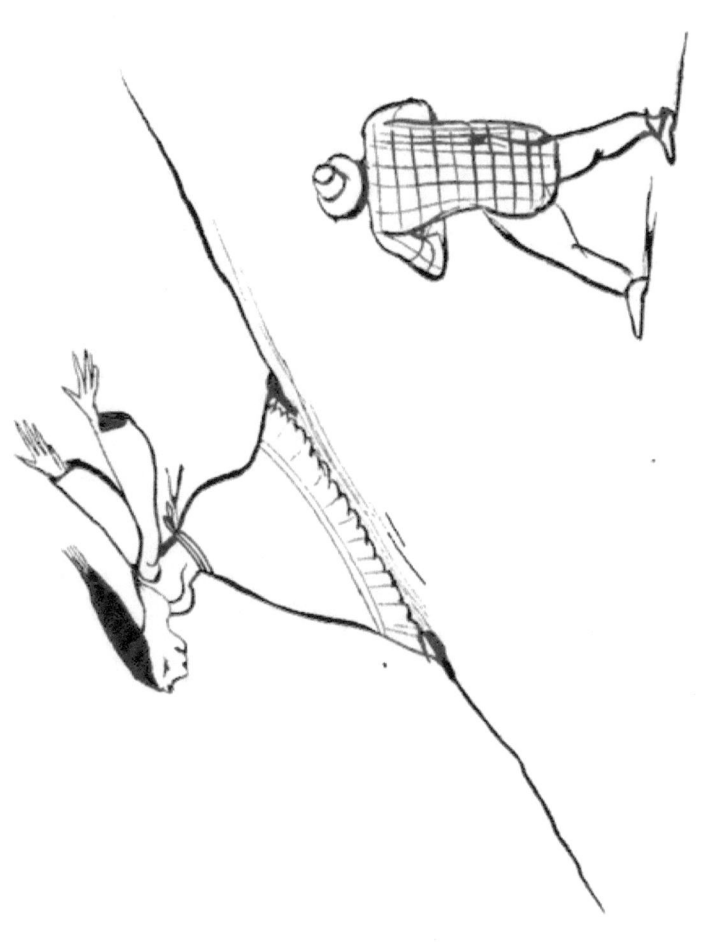

There was an old man of West Dumpet,
Who possessed a large nose like a trumpet;
When he blew it aloud, it astonished the crowd,
And was heard through the whole of West Dumpet.

There was an old man of the Dargle
Who purchased six barrels of Gargle;
For he said, "I'll sit still, And will roll them down hill,
For the fish in the depths of the Dargle."

There was an Old Man at a Junction,
Whose feelings were wrung with compunction,
When they said "The Train's gone!" He exclaimed "How forlorn!"
But remained on the rails of the Junction.

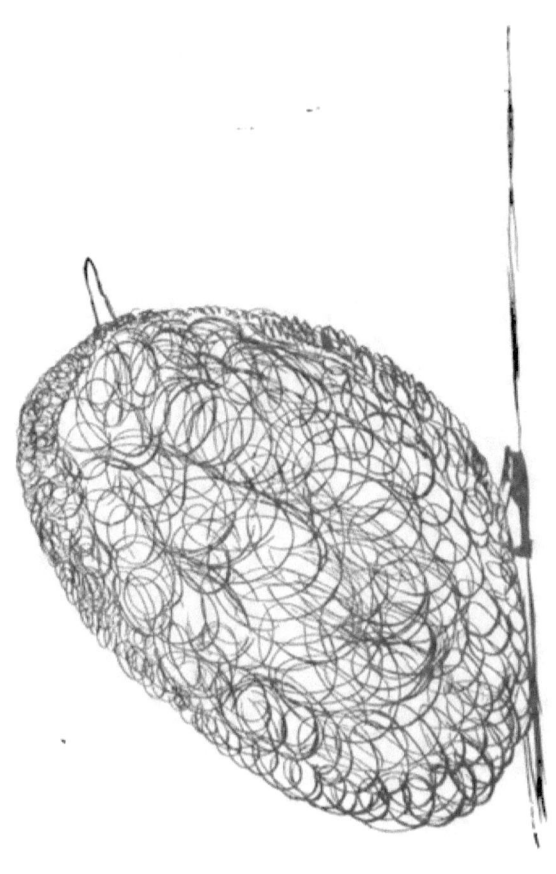

There was an old man of Hong Kong,
Who never did anything wrong;
He lay on his back, with his head in a sack,
That innocuous old man of Hong Kong.

There was an old person of Bar,
Who passed all her life in a jar,
Which she painted pea-green, to appear more serene,
That placid old person of Bar.

There was an old man of Messina,
Whose daughter was named Opsibeena;
She wore a small wig, and rode out on a pig,
To the perfect delight of Messina.

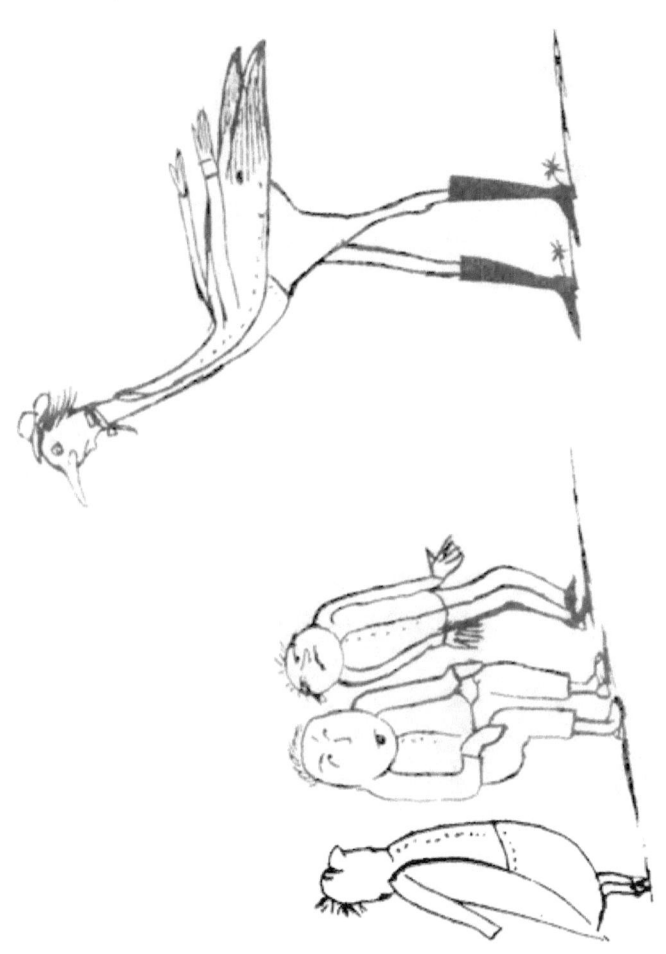

There was an old person of Bromley,
Whose ways were not cheerful or comely;
He sate in the dust, eating spiders and crust,
That unpleasing old person of Bromley.

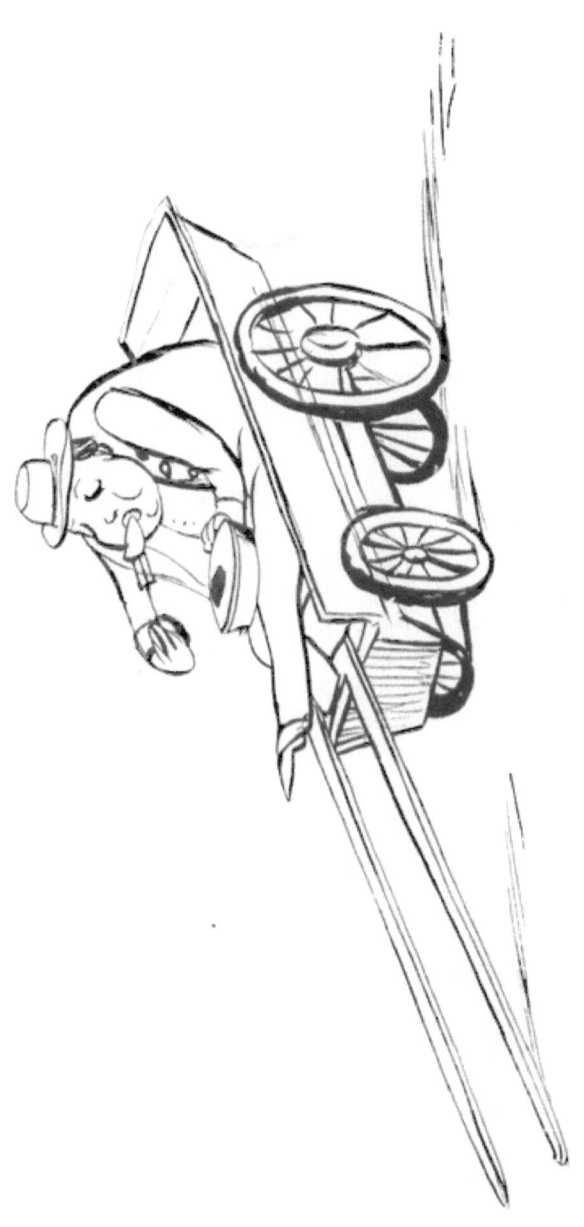

There was a young person of Ayr,
Whose head was remarkably square :
On the top, in fine weather, she wore a gold feather ;
Which dazzled the people of Ayr.

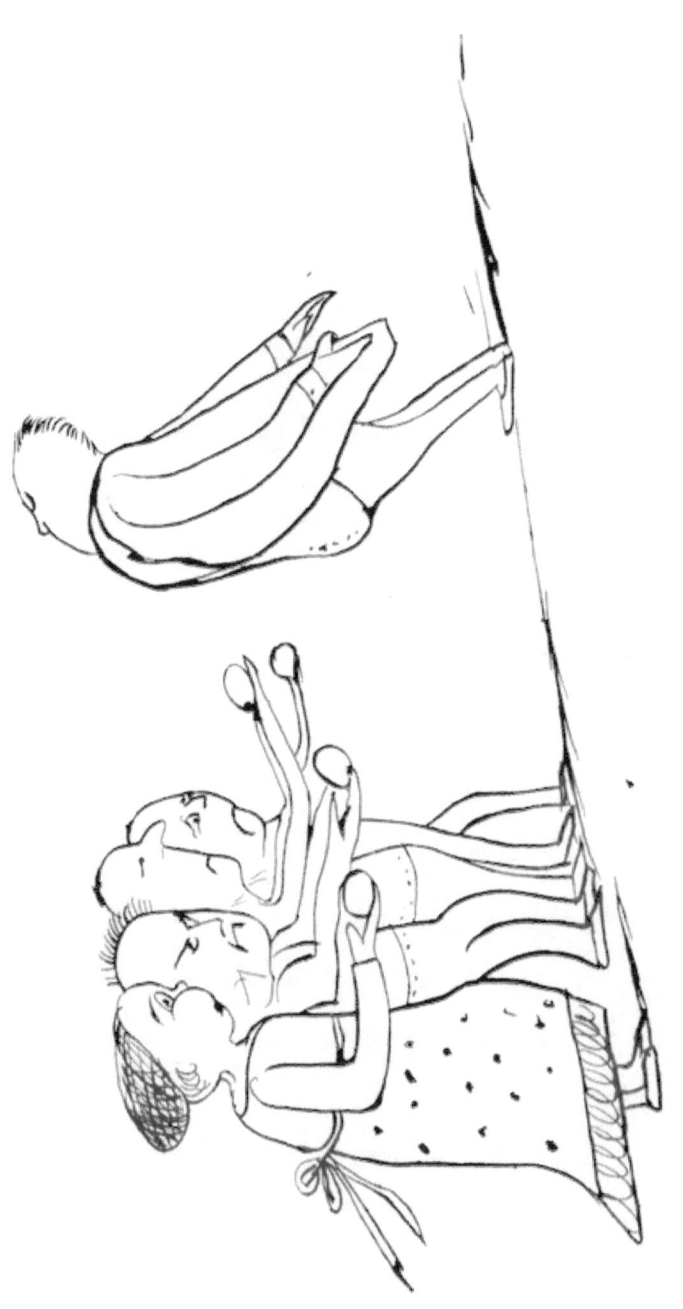

The Comfortable Confidential Cow,
who sate in her Red Morocco Arm Chair and
toasted her own Bread at the parlour Fire.

There was an old man of Blackheath,
Whose head was adorned with a wreath,
Of lobsters and spice, pickled onions and mice,
That uncommon old man of Blackheath,

The Melodious Meritorious Mouse, who played a merry minuet on the Piano-forte.

The Nutritious Newt,
who purchased a Round Plum-pudding
for his grand-daughter.

The Tumultuous Tom-tommy Tortoise,
who beat a Drum all day long in the
middle of the wilderness.

The Zigzag Zealous Zebra, who carried five Monkeys on his back all the way to Jellibolee.

The Obsequious Ornamental Ostrich,
who wore Boots to keep his
feet quite dry.

There was an old person of Ware,
Who rode on the back of a bear:
When they ask'd,—"Does it trot?—he said "Certainly not!
He's a Moppsikon Floppsikon bear!

There was a young lady of Greenwich,
Whose garments were border'd with Spinach ;
But a large spotty Calf, bit her shawl quite in half,
Which alarmed that young lady of Greenwich.

There was a young person in red,
Who carefully covered her head,
With a bonnet of leather, and three lines of feather.
Besides some long ribands of red.

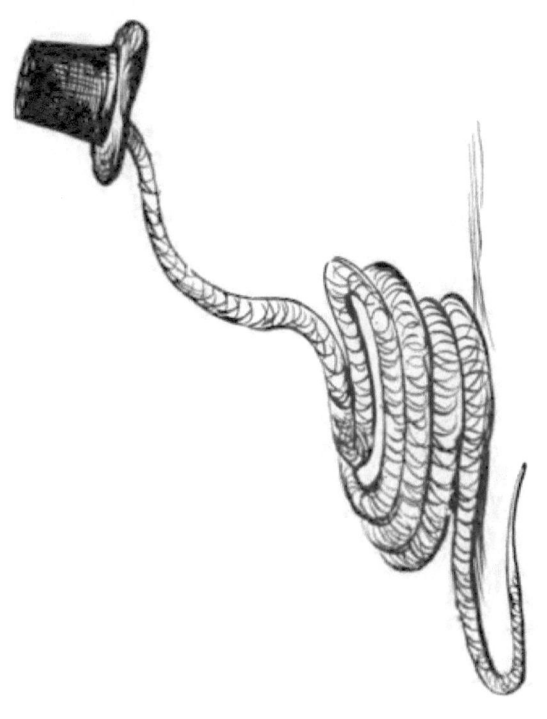

The Scroobious Snake,
who always wore a Hat on his Head, for
fear he should bite anybody.

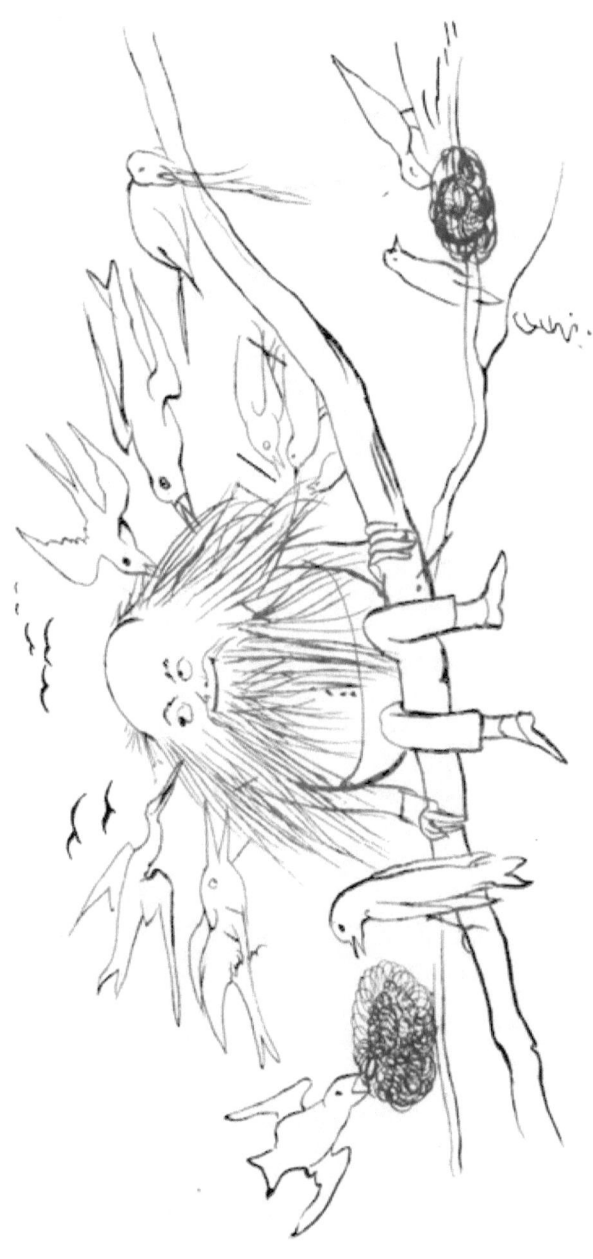

There was an old man in a tree,
Whose whiskers were lovely to see;
But the birds of the air, pluck'd them perfectly bare.
To make themselves nests in that tree.

The Visibly Vicious Vulture,
who wrote some Verses to a Veal-cutlet in a
Volume bound in Vellum.

There was an old man whose despair
Induced him to purchase a hare:
Whereon one fine day, he rode wholly away,
Which partly assuaged his despair.

There was an old person of Hyde,
Who walked by the shore with his bride,
'Till a Crab who came near, fill'd their bosoms with fear,
And they said, " Would we'd never left Hyde!"

The Inventive Indian,
who caught a Remarkable Rabbit in a
Stupendous Silver Spoon.

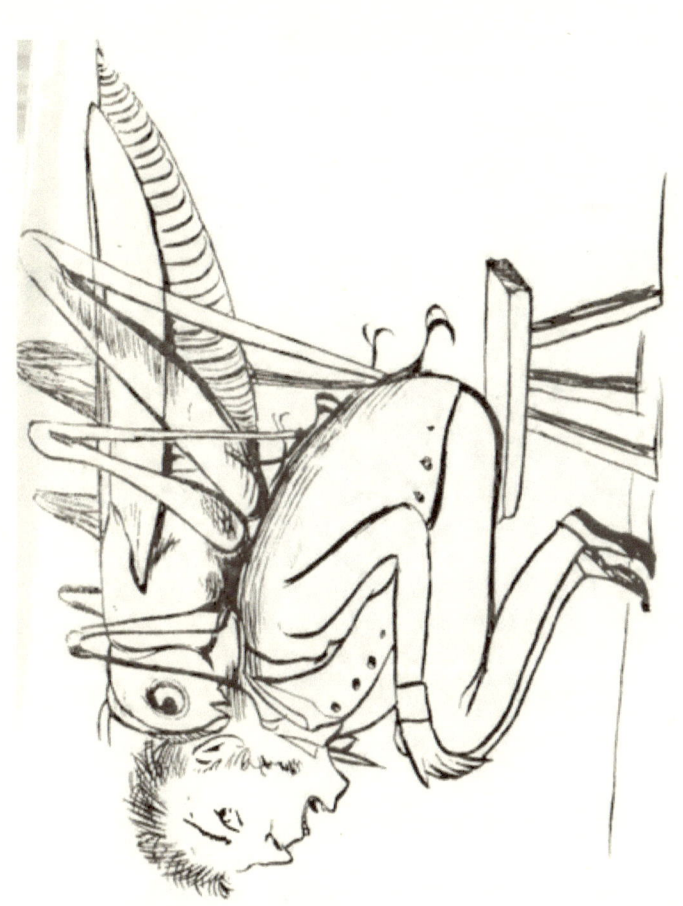

There was an old man in a Marsh,
Whose manners were futile and harsh;
He sate on a log, and sang songs to a frog,
That instructive old man in a Marsh.

TWENTY-SIX NONSENSE RHYMES AND PICTURES.

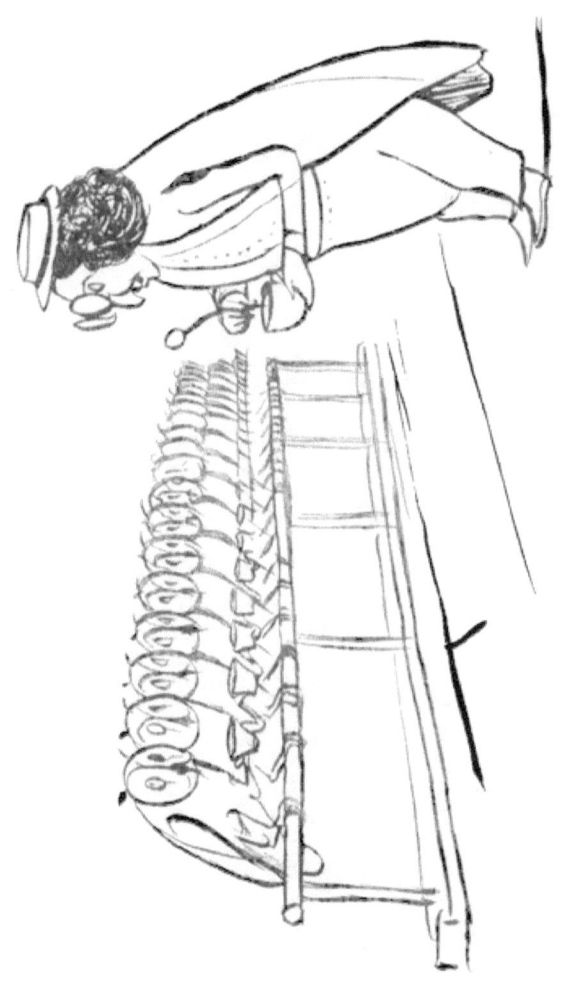

There was an old man of Dumbree,
Who taught little owls to drink tea ;
For he said, " To eat mice, is not proper or nice,"
That amiable man of Dumbree.

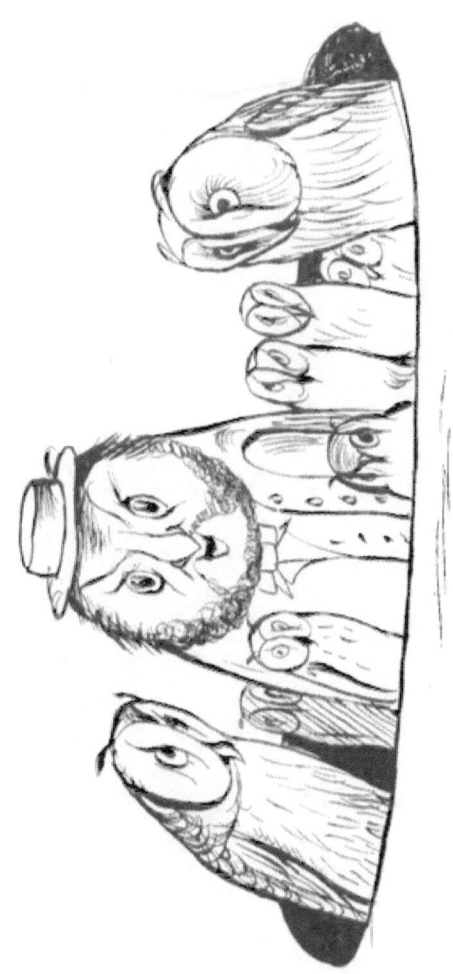

There was an old person of Crowle,
Who lived in the nest of an owl;
When they screamed in the nest, he screamed out with the rest,
That depressing old person of Crowle.

The Goodnatured Grey Gull,
who carried the Old Owl, and his Crimson Carpet-bag.
across the river, because he could not swim.

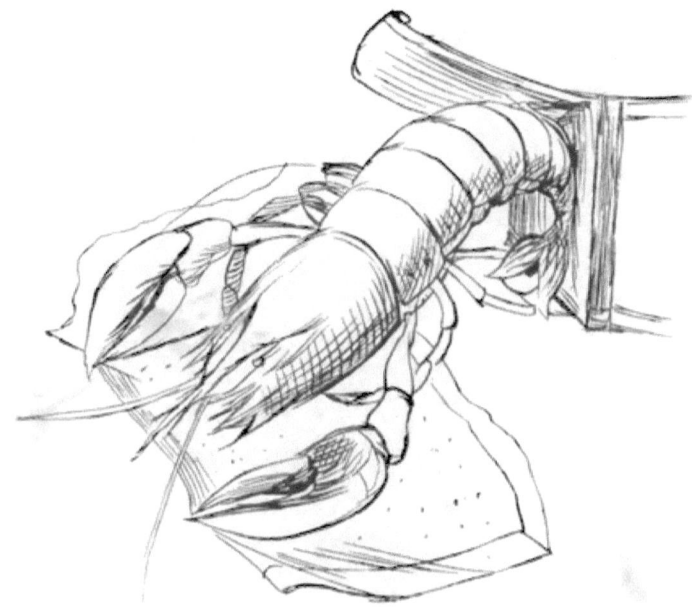

The Lively Learned Lobster,
who mended his own Clothes with
a Needle and Thread.

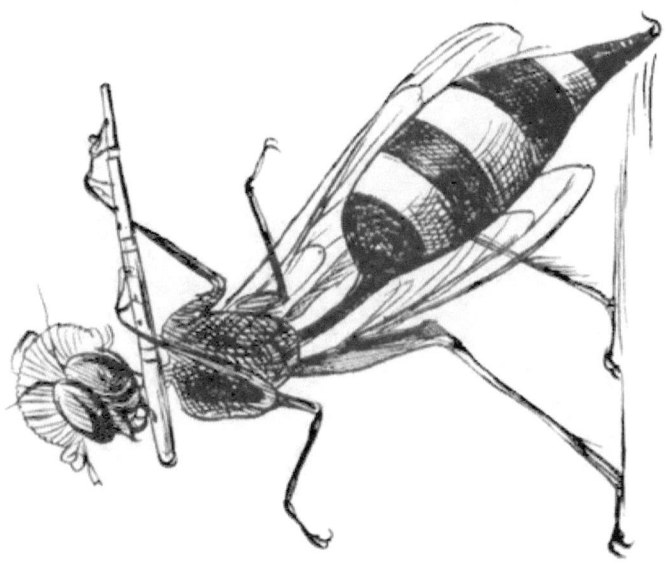

The Worrying Whizzing Wasp,
who stood on a Table, and played sweetly on a
Flute with a Morning Cap.

The Bountiful Beetle,
who always carried a Green Umbrella when it didn't rain,
and left it at home when it did.

There was a young lady in white,
Who looked out at the depths of the night;
But the birds of the air, filled her heart with despair,
And oppressed that young lady in white.

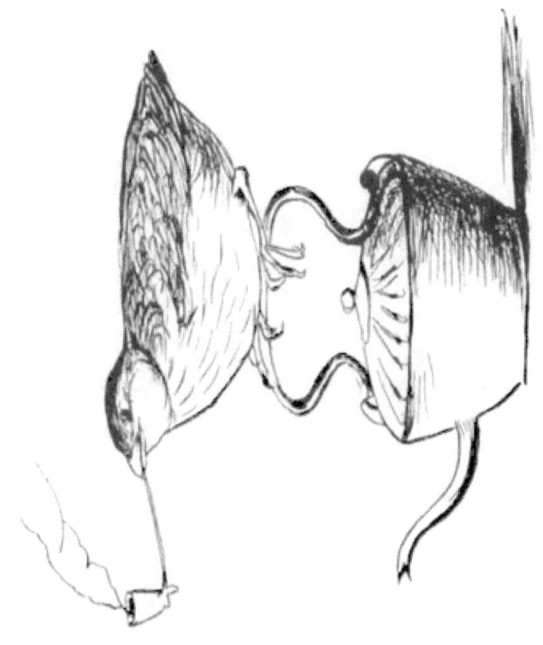

The Queer Querulous Quail, who smoked a Pipe of tobacco on the top of a Tin Tea-kettle.

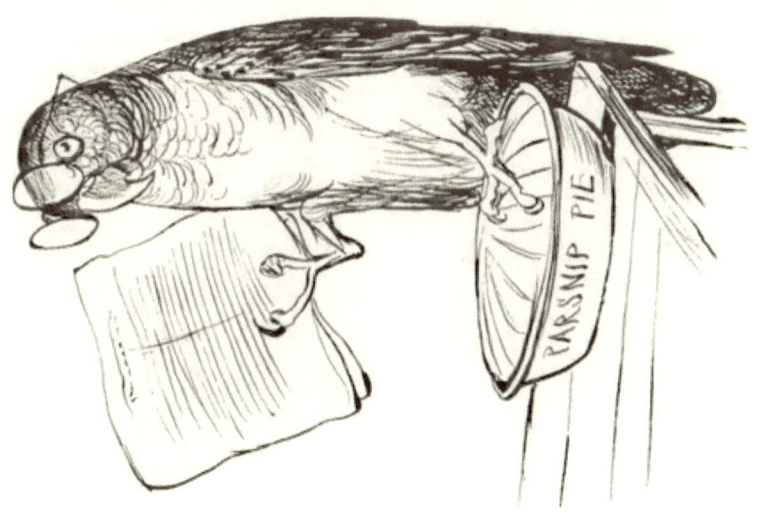

There was an old person of Hove,
Who frequented the depths of a grove ;
Where he studied his books, with the wrens and the rooks,
That tranquil old person of Hove.

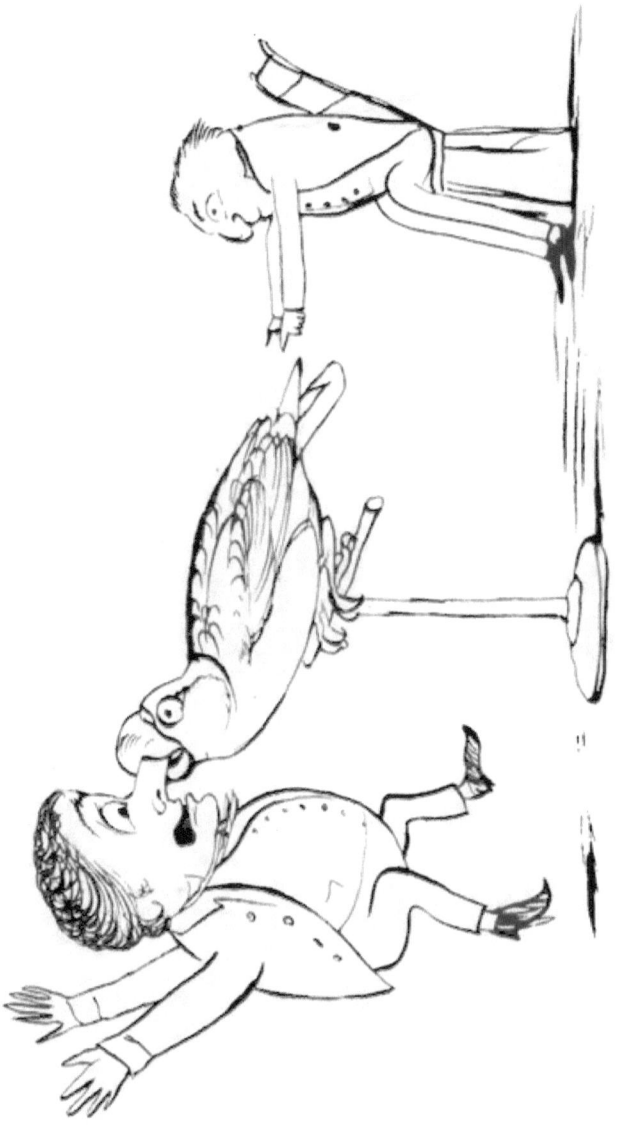

There was an old man of Dunrose ;
A parrot seized hold of his nose.
When he grew melancholy, They said, " His name's Polly,"
Which soothed that old man of Dunrose.

The Rural Runcible Raven,
who wore a White Wig and flew away
with the Carpet Broom.

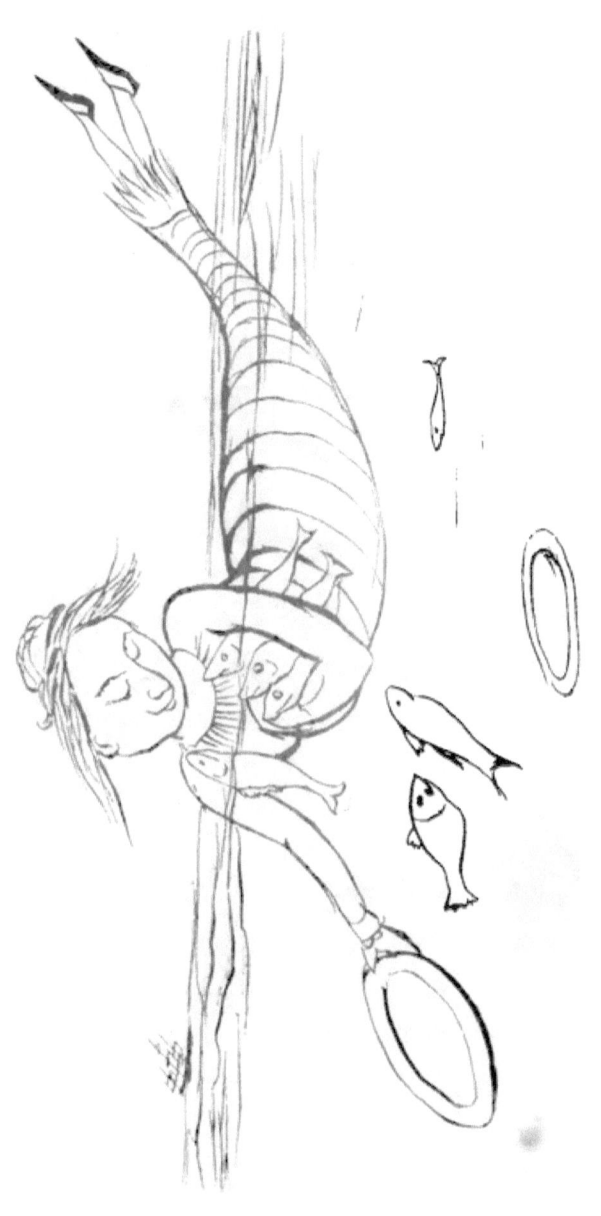

The Hasty Higgeldipiggledy Hen,
who went to market in a Blue Bonnet and Shawl,
and bought a Fish for her Supper.

The Dolomphious Duck,
who caught Spotted Frogs for her dinner
with a Runcible Spoon.

There was an old person of Cannes,
Who purchased three fowls and a fan;
Those she placed on a stool, and to make them feel cool
She constantly fanned them at Cannes.

There was an old person of Nice,
Whose associates were usually Geese.
They walked out together, in all sorts of weather.
That affable person of Nice!

There was an old lady of France,
Who taught little ducklings to dance;
When she said, "Tick-a-tack!"—They only said, "Quack!"
Which grieved that old lady of France.

There was an old person of Florence,
Who held mutton chops in abhorrence;
He purchased a Bustard, and fried him in Mustard,
Which choked that old person of Florence.

The Judicious Jubilant Jay,
who did up her Back Hair every morning with a Wreath of Roses,
Three feathers, and a Gold Pin.

www.ingramcontent.com/pod-product-compliance
Lightning Source LLC
Chambersburg PA
CBHW020858020726
47497CB00005B/1464